an illustrated song for children

BY CYNTHIA TODD

If you haven't heard the "Sing Me a Song Series" by Cynthia Todd, your students are missing a real treat!

European Music Educators Association

Cynthia Todd's "Sing Me a Song Series" is a collection of imaginative, easy to sing story songs. From "Nessie" to the "Heidelberg Castle", Cynthia is successful in touching the hearts and the imagination of children.

Dr. Barbara Elter, Former Music Coordinator,
Dept. of Defense Schools, Germany

Take One Hand is being sung each year schoolwide for Martin Luther King Day. Thank you, Cynthia Todd.

Anne Hollingsworth
McGlone Elementary School,
Denver, Colorado

Cynthia Todd's Music has captivated not only the students but teachers and parents as well. Her songs have a tremendous appeal from Kindergarten to 5th and 6th grades. Heidelberg Castle is a smash!

Sharon Morgenstern
Frankfurt International School

My Media Center would not be complete without the "Sing Me a Song" music corner! Wearing headsets, the kids have no idea how they sound singing Cynthia Todd's songs aloud! Her books and tapes are checked out continuously throughout the year.

Mary Ellen Cravatta, Mark Twain Elementary School
Heidelberg, Germany

Cynthia Todd is an educator, songwriter, singer and performer. Her music is published in the *Silver Burdett World of Music* (Simon & Schuster) and the *"Sing Me a Song Series"* is published exclusively by Alpenhorn Press. She strives to bring children closer to their own imaginative source and develop a deeper sensitivity for all of life. Cynthia shares her teaching, writing and living time in Garmisch, Germany and Sedona, Arizona.

Recommended by The European Educators Association
The National Learning Laboratory – USA

ALPENHORN PRESS • P.O. BOX 1635 • UNIONTOWN PENNSYLVANIA 15401
ISBN 1-879056-12-7

ABC rappin' zebra

an illustrated song for children

Written by Cynthia Todd
Illustrated by Cassandra Johnston
Creative Activities by Debra K. Ziemann

Published by Alpenhorn Press
Box 1635, Uniontown,
Pennsylvania 15401

Designed by Gopa Design

Printed in Seoul, Korea

by

Ulchi Gracom Ltd.

E-mail:GUNNGOOK @hitel.net

There lives a rappin' Zebra
I know her well.
She has a crazy story she loves to tell.
She'll introduce some animals
you may not have met.
Beginning with A in the Alphabet
...let's go!

There once was an ANT who swallowed a BEAR
To swallow a BEAR is extremely rare.
Said the CAT to the DOG, "You better beware!"

As once an EEL I heard say to a FROG,
"A GOAT is quite tasty, but I prefer HOG!

Unless, of course, you come upon a
Glittering, slithering six foot IGUANA
Of which there's enough for you if you wanna!"

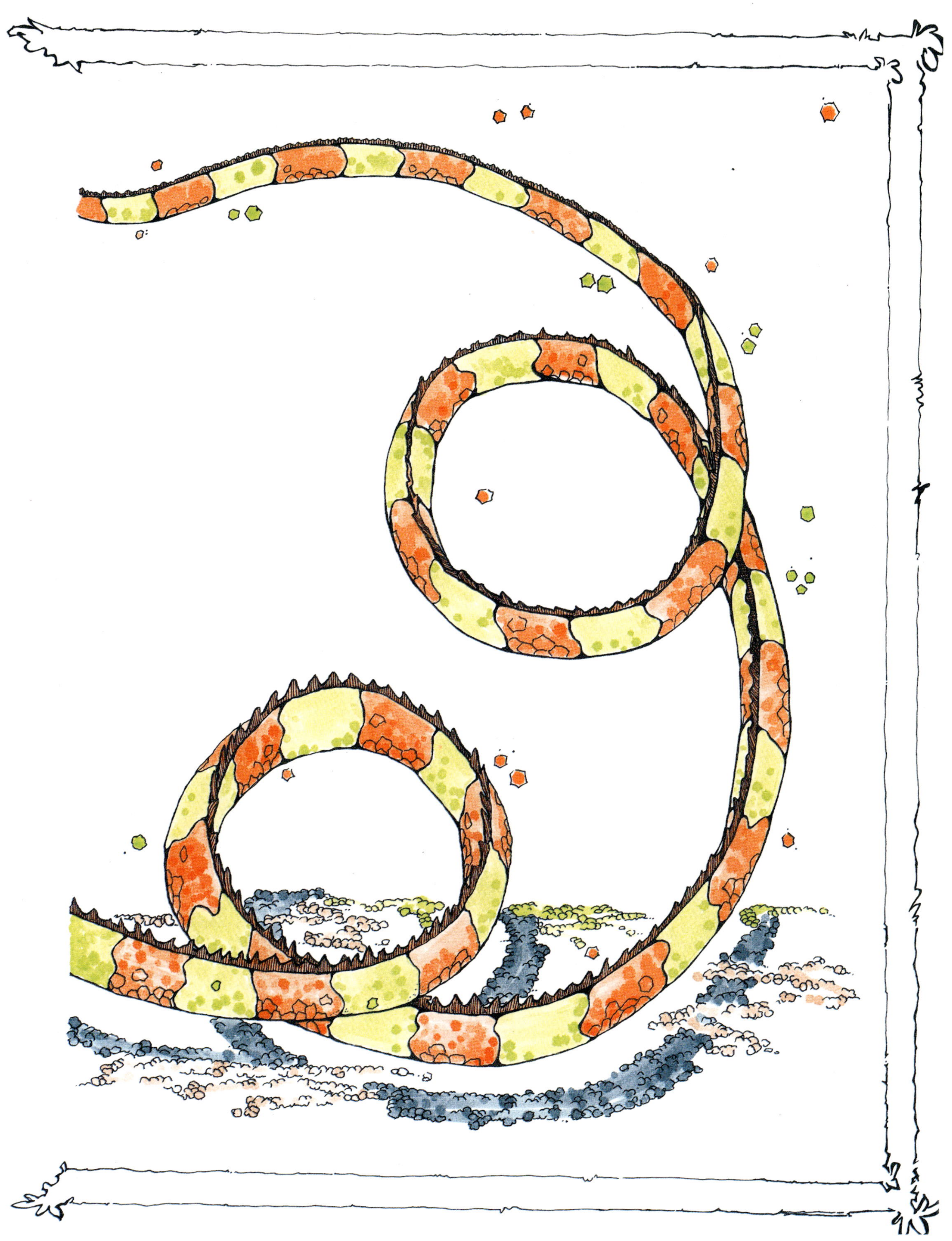

Now you might think this funny but I know it's true,
A JAGUAR who dined with a KANGAROO
In the jungle on Sunday for tea at two.

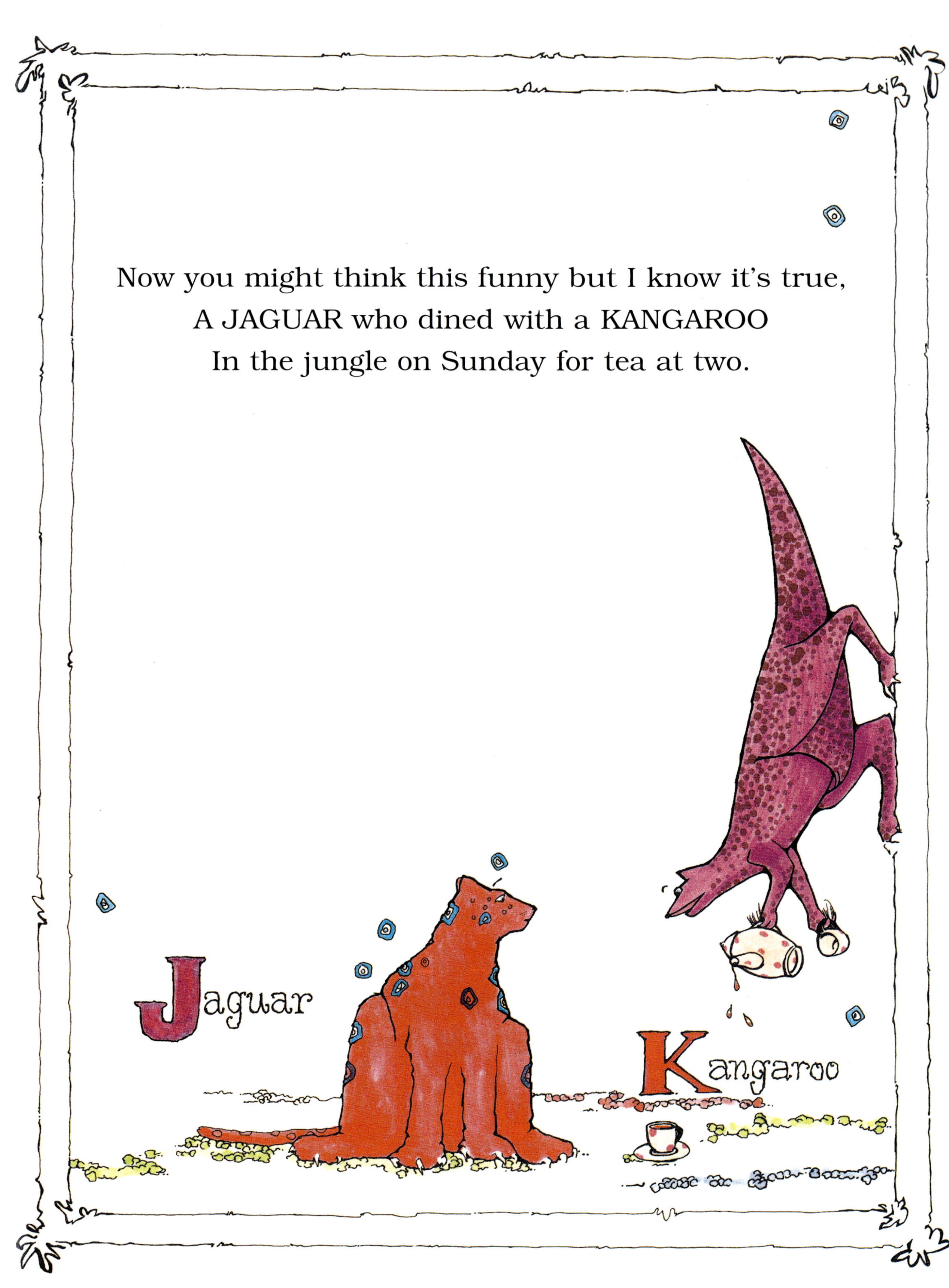

To feast with a LION might leave them both cryin'
Now what do you suppose the LION would do
If he were hungrier for more than just tea for two?

I, too, have a notion, deep in the ocean
MACKEREL and NUMBFISH can make a commotion
When downward they whirl, and downward they swirl
Surrounding the OYSTER to capture her pearl.

When she dresses herself delightfully sweet,
She makes an ideal dish for a PORPOISE to eat.

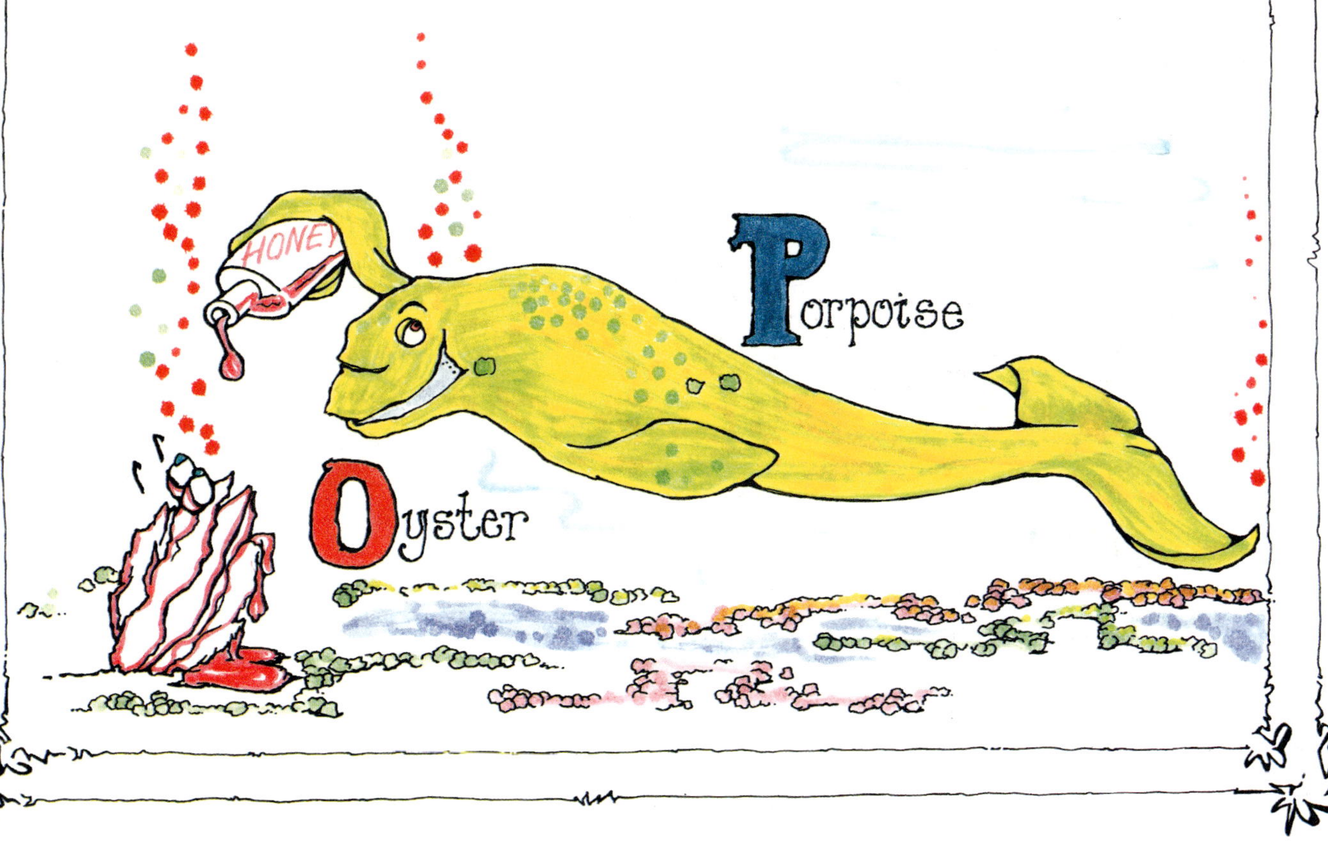

And have you heard the tale of the QUAIL,
Who once tried to nibble on a RACCOON's tail?
"Simply amazing!", cried the conical SNAIL,
Even the TURTLE came out of his shell.

Now what was it that had only one horn?
I believe it was the UNICORN.
A proud animal, indeed it is known,
Surely a VULTURE would leave it alone.

And the WASP and Mr. X, (Who could that be?)
"Neither one should be bothered, you see.

"Don't try to attack it, capture or smack it!",
Says the YELLOWJACKET emphatically.

Now I'd like to say before I close
This might be true but no one knows.
Yet this is the way the story goes
And the only one, I mean the only one,
I said the only one the ZEBRA knows!

The End

ACTIVITIES

THE FOLLOWING ACTIVITIES ARE SUGGESTED for use in the classroom or in the home to provide additional educational experiences while learning the song.

- ❖ Name as many animals as you can that begin with each letter of the alphabet.

- ❖ Make an alphabetical animal mobile.
  Choose your favorite animals and illustrate each one on a
  3" x 5" card (or use different shapes!).
  Put the picture on one side and the letter on the other side of the card.

- ❖ Make a book of your own favorite animals.
  Write a sentence about each one of your animals.

- ❖ Cut out animal pictures from magazines. Group them by beginning letters.

- ❖ Make a list of 4 legged animals and 2 legged animals.
  Group the animals by the number of legs.

- ❖ Make a colorful bar graph in your classroom showing the
  distribution of children's pets.

- ❖ Stand up against the wall. Walk until you think you have walked the length
  of a 6-foot iguana. Measure it to see how well you estimated the length.

- ❖ In a race, which of the animals in the book could you beat?

- ❖ Talk about the different kinds of bears. (Polar, Panda, Koala, etc.)

- ❖ Make a list of creatures with fur, creatures with feathers, and creatures with scales.
  Which animals do not fit in any category?

- ❖ Predict which animals in this story might be friends.

- ❖ Give each animal a name that begins with the same letter.
  For example: Andrew Ant, Bartholomew Bear.

- ❖ Think of a word that describes how each animal might feel.
  Begin each word with the same letter of the alphabet.
  For example: Cranky Cat, Hungry Hog, Tired Turtle.

- ❖ Tell which animal in the story you would like to have for a pet. Why?

- ❖ Which animal in the story would your mother least like you to bring home? Why?

NOW
TURN
THE
BOOK
AROUND

GARDEN PARTY

AN ILLUSTRATED SONG FOR CHILDREN

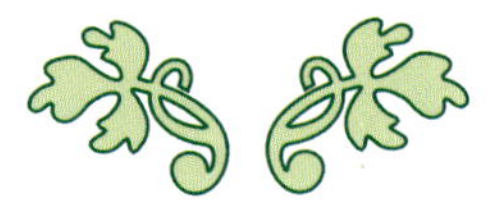

BY CYNTHIA TODD

If you haven't heard the "Sing Me a Song Series" by Cynthia Todd, your students are missing a real treat!

European Music Educators Association

Cynthia Todd's "Sing Me a Song Series" is a collection of imaginative, easy to sing story songs. From "Nessie" to the "Heidelberg Castle", Cynthia is successful in touching the hearts and the imagination of children.

Dr. Barbara Elter, Former Music Coordinator, Dept. of Defense Schools, Germany

Mother Earth is now a play. Take One Hand is being sung each year schoolwide for Martin Luther King Day. Thank you, Cynthia Todd.

Anne Hollingsworth
McGlone Elementary School, Denver, Colorado

Cynthia Todd's Music has captivated not only the students but teachers and parents as well. Her songs have a tremendous appeal from Kindergarten to 5th and 6th grades. Heidelberg Castle is a smash!

Sharon Morgenstern
Frankfurt International School

My Media Center would not be complete without the "Sing Me a Song" music corner! Wearing headsets, the kids have no idea how they sound singing Cynthia Todd's songs aloud! Her books and tapes are checked out continuously throughout the year.

Mary Ellen Cravatta, Mark Twain Elementary School
Heidelberg, Germany

Cynthia Todd is an educator, songwriter, singer and performer. Her music is published in the *Silver Burdett World of Music* (Simon & Schuster) and the "Sing Me a Song Series" is published exclusively by Alpenhorn Press. She strives to bring children closer to their own imaginative source within and develop a deeper sensitivity for all of life. Cynthia shares her teaching, writing and living time in Garmisch, Germany and Sedona, Arizona.

Recommended by The European Educators Association
The National Learning Laboratory – USA

ALPENHORN PRESS • P.O. BOX 1635 • UNIONTOWN PENNSYLVANIA 15401
ISBN 1-879056-12-7

sing me a song
SERIES

GARDEN PARTY

AN ILLUSTRATED SONG FOR CHILDREN

Written by Cynthia Todd
Illustrated by Cassandra Johnston
Creative Activities by Debra K. Ziemann

Published by Alpenhorn Press
Box 1635, Uniontown,
Pennsylvania 15401

Designed by Gopa Design

Printed in Seoul, Korea

by

Ulchi Gracom Ltd.

E-mail:GUNNGOOK @hitel.net

ONE Watermelon who lived in a garden
Winked at the Pumpkin in the pale moonlight.

TWO Corn Ears, heard someone laughing…

THREE Artichokes had to hang on tight.

"It's a Party, time to hit the music,
It's a Party, time to turn on the light."

"It's a Party," cried the old Cucumber,
Who danced and danced all through the night.

Four Avocados skipped in a circle...

FIVE Tomatoes clapped in time.

Violins and trumpets were playing…

SIX Strawberries ran away from the vine.

"It's a Party, time to hit the music,
It's a Party, time to turn on the light."

"It's a Party," cried the old Cucumber,
Who danced and danced all through the night.

SEVEN Zucchinis swayed in the wind with...

EIGHT Green Onions left and right.

NINE Cauliflowers couldn't believe it...

TEN Cabbage Heads rolled out of sight.

"It's a Party, time to hit the music,
It's a Party, time to turn on the light."

"It's a Party," cried the old Cucumber,
Who danced and danced all through the night.

TEN Cabbage Heads,

NINE Cauliflowers,

EIGHT Green Onions in the midnight blue;

SEVEN Zucchinis,

SIX Strawberries,

FIVE Tomatoes heard it too.

"Someone's coming," cried the FOUR Avocados.

"Someone's coming," cried the THREE Artichokes.

"Someone's coming," heard the TWO Corn Ears,

And the ONE Watermelon knew it all was a joke!

"It's a Party, time to hit the music,
It's a Party, time to turn on the light."

"It's a Party," cried the old Cucumber,
Who danced and danced all through the night.

GARDEN PARTY

WORDS AND MUSIC BY
Cynthia Todd

C   G   C
4. F   C
one wat - er mel - lon knew it
G7   C   F   C
all was a joke. It's a par - ty, _____ time to hit the mu - sic. It's a
F   C   G7   C   F   C
par - ty, time to turn on the light. __ It's a par - ty cried the
C   F   C   G7   C
old cu - cum - ber, who danced and danced all thru __ the night. __ It's a
F   C   F   C
par - ty, time to hit the mus - ic. It's a par - ty, time to
G7   C   F   C
turn on the light. __ It's a par - ty cried the old cu - cum - ber, who
F   C   G7   C
danced and danced all thru _______ the night.

Garden Party
A C T I V I T I E S

THE FOLLOWING ACTIVITIES ARE SUGGESTED for use in the classroom or in the home to provide additional educational experiences while learning the song. These activities have been grouped by subject into the following sections: Math, Language Arts, Science, Social Studies, Art, and Creative Writing.

Math

❖ Take a survey of the class's favorite and least favorite vegetable.
   Make two bar graphs to show the results.

❖ Take a survey of the class's favorite and least favorite fruit.
   Make two picture graphs to show the results.

❖ Have each child bring in a fruit or vegetable.
   Put the children into small groups and have them write one
   and two part story problems using the fruits and vegetables as the subject.

Language Arts

❖ Classroom Play:
   a. Choose one student as a representative for each fruit and
      vegetable in the song Garden Party.

   b. Have each representative cut out as many pieces of their fruit or
      vegetable as appear in the song. Pin the pieces onto the child.
      (ex. The child representing the strawberries will have six strawberries
      pinned to her/him).

   c. The students who are not characters will sing the song as the fruits
      and vegetables act out the song.

Science

❖ Brainstorm and list as many fruits and vegetables as the children can.
   Classify them by colors.

❖ Plant a lima bean seed and chart it's growth.

❖ Discuss the four food groups and the importance of fruits and vegetables.

❖ Have each child bring in a piece of fruit. (Try to get a wide variety!) Select a seed from each different piece of fruit and study it carefully. Discover how the various seeds are alike and different.

Art

❖ Search through magazines for pictures of fruits and vegetables. Make a fruit and vegetable collage.

❖ Make a mobile with three dimensional "partying" fruits and vegetables.
   a. Cut two identical pieces for each fruit/vegetable.

   b. Staple the perimeter of the two pieces together leaving an opening big enough to stuff with newspaper or other paper scraps.

   c. Stuff the fruit/vegetable and staple the opening.

   d. Attach strings of varying lengths to each piece and tie onto a hanger.

   e. Give each piece its own character by adding faces, arms, legs, clothing, etc.

❖ Fruit and Vegetable Printing

❖ Combine the physical characteristics of two or three vegetables to create your "new" vegetable to invite to the Garden Party. Draw it.

Creative Writing

❖ Write a newspaper article to follow this headline: "Five Year Old Boy is Saved By a Watermelon."

❖ Pretend that you are one of the fruits or vegetables at the Garden Party. Give yourself a name. Write a story describing what your life was like BEFORE the Garden Party.

Alpenhorn Press

Presents

Cynthia Todd's

"SING ME A SONG"

Series

Books and Cassette Tapes for Children

★

**Children love the songs
written and sung by Cynthia Todd**

★

Each packaged set contains
2 creatively illustrated activity books
to sing, read and color,
and 1 cassette tape which sings each story.

★

In the back of each book are educational activities
to challenge all ages in a variety of curriculum areas.

★

Featured since 1990 at:

ASSOCIATION FOR THE YOUNG CHILD EUROPE

DISTRICT WIDE YOUNG AUTHORS CONFERENCES

MUSIC EDUCATORS CONFERENCES EUROPE

ELEMENTARY SCHOOL SONGWRITER/AUTHOR
PERFORMANCES

ELEMENTARY EDUCATION WORKSHOPS
AND SCHOOL BOOKFAIRS

★

Recommended by:

EUROPEAN MUSIC EDUCATORS ASSOCIATION

THE NATIONAL LEARNING LABORATORY - USA

★

Suitable for
PRESCHOOL (★)   PRIMARY (★★)   INTERMEDIATE (★★★)

SET 1 ★ ★★ ★★★

$12.95

SET 2 ★ ★★

$12.95

SET 3 ★★ ★★★

$12.95

SET 4 ★ ★★

$12.95

SET 5 ★ ★★

$12.95

SET 6 ★ ★★

Full Color
Hardback

$15.95

ALPENHORN PRESS

PO Box 1635, Uniontown PA 15401 • Phone/Fax: 724 · 438 · 0992
email: dxz5@psu.edu
visit our website! http://www.sni.net/alpenhorn

NOW
TURN
THE
BOOK
AROUND